Watling Park School
Pavilion Way
Burnt Oak
HA8 9YA

Originally published as part of A Chinese Wonder Book in 1919.
Copyright © 2016 Bad Pup Projects.
All rights reserved.
ISBN-10: 1537210750
ISBN-13: 978-1537210759

BAMBOO AND THE TURTLE

by

NORMAN HINSDALE PITMAN

A Chinese Wonder Book is a collection of adapted Chinese folk tales written by Norman Hinsdale Pitman. The tales were originally published in 1919 as a single book.
We have included the original illustrations by Li Chu-T'ang as the cover images for these individual volumes.

Norman Hinsdale Pitman (1876-1925) worked as an English professor at universities in China.

A party of visitors had been seeing the sights at Hsi Ling. They had just passed down the Holy Way between the huge stone animals when Bamboo, a little boy of twelve, son of a temple keeper, rushed out from his father's house to see the mandarins go by. Such a parade of great men he had never seen before, even on the feast days. There were ten sedan chairs, with bearers dressed in flaming colours, ten long-handled, red umbrellas, each carried far in front of its proud owner, and a long line of horsemen.

When this gay procession had filed past, Bamboo was almost ready to cry because he could not run after the sightseers as they went from temple to temple and from tomb to tomb. But, alas! His father had ordered him never to follow tourists. "If you do, they will take you for a beggar, Bamboo," he had said shrewdly, "and if you're a beggar, then your daddy's one too. Now they don't want any beggars around the royal tombs." So Bamboo had never known the pleasure of pursuing the rich. Many times he had turned back to the little mud house, almost broken-hearted at seeing his playmates running, full of glee, after the great men's chairs.

On the day when this story opens, just as the last horseman had passed out of sight among the cedars, Bamboo chanced to look up toward one of the smaller temple buildings of which his father was the keeper. It was the house through which the visitors had just been shown. Could his eyes be deceiving him? No, the great iron doors had been forgotten in the hurry of the moment, and there they stood wide open, as if inviting him to enter.

In great excitement he scurried toward the temple. How often he had pressed his head against the bars and looked into the dark room, wishing and hoping that some day he might go in. And yet, not once had he been granted this favour. Almost every day since babyhood he had gazed at the high stone shaft, or tablet, covered with Chinese writing, that stood in the centre of the lofty room, reaching almost to the roof. But with still greater surprise his eyes had feasted on the giant turtle underneath, on whose back the column rested. There are many such tablets to be seen in China, many such turtles patiently bearing their loads of stone, but this was the only sight of the kind that Bamboo had seen. He had never been outside the Hsi Ling forest, and, of course, knew very little of the great world beyond.

It is no wonder then that the turtle and the tablet had always astonished him. He had asked his father to explain the mystery. "Why do they have a turtle? Why not a lion or an elephant?" For he had seen stone figures of these animals in the park and had thought them much better able than his friend, the turtle, to carry loads on their backs.

"Why it's just the custom," his father had replied—the answer always given when Bamboo asked a question, "just the custom." The boy had tried to imagine it all for himself, but had never been quite sure that he was right, and now, joy of all joys, he was about to enter the very turtle-room itself. Surely, once inside, he could find some answer to this puzzle of his childhood.

Breathless, he dashed through the doorway, fearing every minute that someone would notice the open gates and close them before he could enter. Just in front of the giant turtle he fell in a little heap on the floor, which was covered inch-deep with dust. His face was streaked, his clothes were a sight to behold; but Bamboo cared nothing for such trifles. He lay there for a few moments, not daring to move. Then, hearing a noise outside, he crawled under the ugly stone beast and crouched in his narrow hiding-place, as still as a mouse.

"There, there!" said a deep voice. "See what you are doing, stirring up such a dust! Why, you will strangle me if you are not careful."
It was the turtle speaking, and yet Bamboo's father had often told him that it was not alive. The boy lay trembling for a minute, too much frightened to get up and run.

"No use in shaking so, my lad," the voice continued, a little more kindly. "I suppose all boys are alike—good for nothing but kicking up a dust." He finished this sentence with a hoarse chuckle, and the boy, seeing that he was laughing, looked up with wonder at the strange creature.

"I meant no harm in coming," said the child finally. "I only wanted to look at you more closely."

"Oh, that was it, hey? Well, that is strange. All the others come and stare at the tablet on my back. Sometimes they read aloud the nonsense written there about dead emperors and their titles, but they never so much as look at me, at me whose father was one of the great four who made the world."

Bamboo's eyes shone with wonder. "What! Your father helped make the world?" he gasped.

"Well, not my father exactly, but one of my grandfathers, and it amounts to the same thing, doesn't it. But, hark! I hear a voice. The keeper is coming back. Run up and close those doors, so he won't notice that they have not been locked. Then you may hide in the corner there until he has passed. I have something more to tell you."

Bamboo did as he was told. It took all his strength to swing the heavy doors into place. He felt very important to think that he was doing something for the grandson of a maker of the world, and it would have broken his heart if this visit had been ended just as it was beginning.

Sure enough, his father and the other keepers passed on, never dreaming that the heavy locks were not fastened as usual. They were talking about the great men who had just gone. They seemed very happy and were jingling some coins in their hands.

"Now, my boy," said the stone turtle when the sound of voices had died away and Bamboo had come out from his corner, "maybe you think I'm proud of my job. Here I've been holding up this chunk for a hundred years, I who am fond of travel. During all this time night and day, I have been trying to think of some way to give up my position. Perhaps it's honourable, but, you may well imagine, it's not very pleasant."

"I should think you would have the backache," ventured Bamboo timidly.

"Backache! Well, I think so; back, neck, legs, eyes, everything I have is aching, aching for freedom. But, you see, even if I had kicked up my heels and overthrown this monument, I had no way of getting through those iron bars," and he nodded toward the gate.

"Yes, I understand," agreed Bamboo, beginning to feel sorry for his old friend.

"But, now that you are here, I have a plan, and a good one it is, too, I think. The watchmen have forgotten to lock the gate. What is to prevent my getting my freedom this very night? You open the gate, I walk out, and no one the wiser."

"But my father will lose his head if they find that he has failed to do his duty and you have escaped."

"Oh, no; not at all. You can slip his keys to-night, lock the gates after I am gone, and no one will know just what has happened. Why it will make this building famous. It won't hurt your father, but will do him good. So many travellers will be anxious to see the spot from which I vanished. I am too heavy for a thief to carry off, and they will be sure that it is another miracle of the gods. Oh, I shall have a good time out in the big world."

Just here Bamboo began to cry.

"Now what is the silly boy blubbering about?" sneered the turtle. "Is he nothing but a cry-baby?"

"No, but I don't want you to go."

"Don't want me to go, eh? Just like all the others. You're a fine fellow! What reason have you for wanting to see me weighed down here all the rest of my life with a mountain on my back? Why, I thought you were sorry for me, and it turns out that you are as mean as anybody else."

"It is so lonely here, and I have no playmates. You are the only friend I have."

The tortoise laughed loudly. "Ho, ho! So it's because I make you a good playmate, eh? Now, if that's your reason, that's another story altogether. What do you say to going with me then? I, too, need a friend, and if you help me to escape, why, you are the very friend for me."

"But how shall you get the tablet off your back?" questioned Bamboo doubtfully. "It's very heavy."

"That's easy, just walk out of the door. The tablet is too tall to go through. It will slide off and sit on the floor instead of on my shell." Bamboo, wild with delight at the thought of going on a journey with the turtle, promised to obey the other's commands. After supper, when all were asleep in the little house of the keeper, he slipped from his bed, took down the heavy key from its peg, and ran pell-mell to the temple.

"Well, you didn't forget me, did you?" asked the turtle when Bamboo swung the iron gates open.

"Oh, no, I would not break a promise. Are you ready?"

"Yes, quite ready." So saying, the turtle took a step. The tablet swayed backward and forward, but did not fall. On walked the turtle until finally he stuck his ugly head through the doorway. "Oh, how good it looks outside," he said. "How pleasant the fresh air feels! Is that the moon rising over yonder? It's the first time I've seen it for an age. My word! Just look at the trees! How they have grown since they set that tombstone on my back! There's a regular forest outside now."

Bamboo was delighted when he saw the turtle's glee at escaping. "Be careful," he cried, "not to let the tablet fall hard enough to break it."

Even as he spoke, the awkward beast waddled through the door. The upper end of the monument struck against the wall, toppled off, and fell with a great crash to the floor. Bamboo shivered with fear. Would his father come and find out what had happened?

"Don't be afraid, my boy. No one will come at this hour of the night to spy on us."

Bamboo quickly locked the gates, ran back to the house, and hung the key on its peg. He took a long look at his sleeping parents, and then returned to his friend. After all, he would not be gone long and his father would surely forgive him.

Soon the comrades were walking down the broad road, very slowly, for the tortoise is not swift of foot and Bamboo's legs were none too long.

"Where are you going?" said the boy at last, after he had begun to feel more at home with the turtle.

"Going? Where should you think I would want to go after my century in prison? Why, back to the first home of my father, back to the very spot where the great god, P'anku, and his three helpers hewed out the world."

"And is it far?" faltered the boy, beginning to feel just the least bit tired.

"At this rate, yes, but, bless my life, you didn't think we could travel all the way at this snail's pace, I hope. Jump on my back, and I'll show you how to go. Before morning we shall be at the end of the world, or rather, the beginning."

"Where is the beginning of the world?" asked Bamboo. "I have never studied geography."

"We must cross China, then Tibet, and at last in the mountains just beyond we shall reach the spot which P'anku made the centre of his labour."

At that moment Bamboo felt himself being lifted from the ground. At first he thought he would slip off the turtle's rounded shell, and he cried out in fright.

Never fear," said his friend. "Only sit quietly, and there will be no danger."

They had now risen far into the air, and Bamboo could look down over the great forest of Hsi Ling all bathed in moonlight. There were the broad white roads leading up to the royal tombs, the beautiful temples, the buildings where oxen and sheep were prepared for sacrifice, the lofty towers, and the high tree-covered hills under which the emperors were buried. Until that night Bamboo had not known the size of this royal graveyard. Could it be that the turtle would carry him beyond the forest? Even as he asked himself this question he saw that they had reached a mountain, and the turtle was ascending higher, still higher, to cross the mighty wall of stone.

Bamboo grew dizzy as the turtle rose farther into the sky. He felt as he sometimes did when he played whirling games with his little friends, and got so dizzy that he tumbled over upon the ground. However, this time he knew that he must keep his head and not fall, for it must have been almost a mile to the ground below him. At last they had passed over the mountain and were flying above a great plain. Far below Bamboo could see sleeping villages and little streams of water that looked like silver in the moonlight. Now, directly beneath them was a city. A few feeble lights could be seen in the dark narrow streets, and Bamboo thought he could hear the faint cries of peddlers crying their midnight wares.

"That's the capital of Shan-shi just below us," said the turtle, breaking his long silence. "It is almost two hundred miles from here to your father's house, and we have taken less than half an hour. Beyond that is the Province of the Western Valleys. In one hour we shall be above Tibet."

On they whizzed at lightning speed. If it had not been hot summer time Bamboo would have been almost frozen. As it was, his hands and feet were cold and stiff. The turtle, as if knowing how chilly he was, flew nearer to the ground where it was warmer. How pleasant for

Bamboo! He was so tired that he could keep his eyes open no longer and he was soon soaring in the land of dreams.

When he waked up it was morning. He was lying on the ground in a wild, rocky region. Not far away burned a great wood fire, and the turtle was watching some food that was cooking in a pot.

"Ho, ho, my lad! So you have at last waked up after your long ride. You see we are a little early. No matter if the dragon does think he can fly faster, I beat him, didn't I? Why, even the phoenix laughs at me and says I am slow, but the phoenix has not come yet either. Yes, I have clearly broken the record for speed, and I had a load to carry too, which neither of the others had, I am sure."

"Where are we?" questioned Bamboo.

"In the land of the beginning," said the other wisely. "We flew over Tibet, and then went northwest for two hours. If you haven't studied geography you won't know the name of the country. But, here we are, and that is enough, isn't it, enough for any one? And to-day is the yearly feast-day in honour of the making of the world. It was very fortunate for me that the gates were left open yesterday. I am afraid my old friends, the dragon and the phoenix, have almost forgotten what I look like. It is so long since they saw me. Lucky beasts they are, not to be loaded down under an emperor's tablet. Hello! I hear the dragon coming now, if I am not mistaken. Yes, here he is. How glad I am to see him!"

Bamboo heard a great noise like the whirr of enormous wings, and then, looking up, saw a huge dragon just in front of him. He knew it was a dragon from the pictures he had seen and the carvings in the temples.

The dragon and the turtle had no sooner greeted each other, both very happy at the meeting, than they were joined by a queer-looking bird, unlike any that Bamboo had ever seen, but which he knew was the phœnix. This phœnix looked somewhat like a wild swan, but it had the bill of a cock, the neck of a snake, the tail of a fish and the stripes of a dragon. Its feathers were of five colours.

When the three friends had chatted merrily for a few minutes, the turtle told them how Bamboo had helped him to escape from the temple.

"A clever boy," said the dragon, patting Bamboo gently on the back.

"Yes, yes, a clever boy indeed," echoed the phœnix.

"Ah," sighed the turtle, "if only the good god, P'anku, were here, shouldn't we be happy! But, I fear he will never come to this meeting-place. No doubt he is off in some distant spot, cutting out another world. If I could only see him once more, I feel that I should die in peace."

"Just listen!" laughed the dragon. "As if one of us could die! Why, you talk like a mere mortal."

All day long the three friends chatted, feasted, and had a good time looking round at the places where they had lived so happily when P'anku had been cutting out the world. They were good to Bamboo also and showed him many wonderful things of which he had never dreamed.

"You are not half so mean-looking and so fierce as they paint you on the flags," said Bamboo in a friendly voice to the dragon just as they were about to separate.

The three friends laughed heartily.

"Oh, no, he's a very decent sort of fellow, even if he is covered with fish-scales," joked the phœnix.

Just before they bade each other good-bye, the phœnix gave Bamboo a long scarlet tail-feather for a keepsake, and the dragon gave him a large scale which turned to gold as soon as the boy took it into his hand.

"Come, come, we must hurry," said the turtle. "I am afraid your father will think you are lost."

So Bamboo, after having spent the happiest day of his life, mounted the turtle's back, and they rose once more above the clouds. Back they flew even faster than they had come. Bamboo had so many things to talk about that he did not once think of going to sleep, for he had really seen the dragon and the phœnix, and if he never were to see anything else in his life, he would always be happy.

Suddenly the turtle stopped short in his swift flight, and Bamboo felt himself slipping. Too late he screamed for help, too late he tried to save himself. Down, down from that dizzy height he tumbled, turning, twisting, thinking of the awful death that was surely coming. Swish! He shot through the tree tops trying vainly to clutch the friendly branches. Then with a loud scream he struck the ground, and his long journey was ended.

"Come out from under that turtle, boy! What are you doing inside the temple in the dirt? Don't you know this is not the proper place for you?" Bamboo rubbed his eyes. Though only half awake, he knew it was his father's voice.

"But didn't it kill me?" he said as his father pulled him out by the heel from under the great stone turtle.

"What killed you, foolish boy? What can you be talking about? But I'll half-kill you if you don't hurry out of this and come to your supper. Really I believe you are getting too lazy to eat. The idea of sleeping the whole afternoon under that turtle's belly!"

Bamboo, not yet fully awake, stumbled out of the tablet room, and his father locked the iron doors.

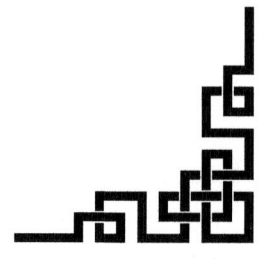

Printed in Great Britain
by Amazon